PUUUNG

편 안 하 고

사랑스럽고

그   래

Love is··· 1

편안하고
사랑스럽고
그   래

Love is··· 1

글·그림 퍼엉

위즈덤하우스

일러스트레이터
퍼엉입니다

'편안하고 사랑스럽고 그래' 시리즈를 그리기 시작한 지 어느덧 5년이 되어갑니다. 이 책의 개정판 소식을 듣고, 저는 한동안 마음이 자주 일렁였어요. 많은 분들께 과분한 사랑을 받아 기쁘고 감사한 날들이 많았지요. 제겐 '첫'이라는 키워드가 참 중요해요. 첫 데이트, 첫 키스, 첫사랑, 나의 모든 '첫'번째. 그래서 저의 첫 책인『편안하고 사랑스럽고 그래』1권 역시 그 의미가 크지요.

5년 전, 사실 이 시리즈의 시작점에 서 있는 퍼엉은 그리 행복한 사람이 아니었어요. 그림이 좋아 애니메이션과에 진학했지만 좋아하는 마음 하나로 버티기엔 제 그림 실력이 출중하지 않다는 것을 잘 알고 있었어요. 그래서 교수님들이 시키는 대로, 무작정 열심히, 많이 그리는 데에만 몰두해 있었어요. 그러다 그림이라면 손가락 하나 까딱하고 싶지 않은 순간을 맞았지요. 그림을 그리는 일이 재미없고 싫어졌어요. 가장 사랑했던 일이 싫어지는 순간이 오면 사람이 참 비참해져요. 행복하지 않아요. '행복하지 않다.' 이 문장 외에는 그 당시 마음을 설명할 길이 없었어요.

저는 이렇게 살 수 없다고 생각했어요. 그리고 하루에 한 장석 나를 위한 그림을 그리자고 마음먹었지요. 아름다운 건축물, 사랑에 빠진 여자와 남자, 고양이. 제가 좋아하는 것들을 모아 그림을 그리기 시작했어요. 비슷한 소재의 그림이 여러 장 모이고, 저는 그 그림들에 '편안하고 사랑스럽고 그래'라는 이름을 붙였지요.

시리즈를 그리는 내내 사랑이라는 감정에 집중하면서 스스로 많은 위로를 받았어요. '삶을 살아 낸다'는 문장을 떠올리면 행복, 즐거움, 기쁨과 같은 감정보단, 숨이 막힌다는 느낌이 강하게 들 때가 있지요. 사랑은 제게 '그럼에도'와 같은 부사와 같다는 것을 깨달았어요. 사는 게 지치고 힘든데, 그럼에도 불구하고 나를 행복하고, 기쁘고, 감사하게 만드는 것. 제겐 그것이 사랑이었어요. 제게 위로가 되었던 이 그림들이 여러분에게도 위로가 되었으면 좋겠어요.

I am Puuung,

an illustrator

It has been almost 5 years unawares since I started painting illustrations titled 'Love is...' series. When I was informed of issuing a revised edition of this illustration book, my heart had often been touched for a fairly long time. Many people have loved my illustrations than they deserved, so I have spent my days, being happy with it and appreciating it. For me, 'first' is a very important keyword. All first things of mine including my first date, my first kiss, my first love... The first volume of this series is also meaningful to me.

Actually, Puuung was not a very happy person at the start of this series. I loved painting and majored in animation at university. But I knew that I wasn't endowed with painting enough to continue to paint and build my career as an illustrator only with my passion for it. I was absorbed in drawing a lot, blindly, and diligently as my professors taught me. Then I came up against the time that I disliked moving any finger for painting. I lost interest in my painting and even hated it. If you hated the most favorite job, you would be miserable. You would not be happy. I can't describe my feelings then except this simple sentence: "I'm not happy."

I thought that I shouldn't live like this, and I decided to paint an illustration for my own sake every day. Beautiful buildings, a woman and a man in love, a cat... I began painting my favorite things. Several illustrations from similar materials had piled up, and I gave a title 'Love is...' to them.

I felt a lot of comfort while I concentrated on the feeling of love throughout the entire time I painted this series. When I'm reminded the phrase 'live a life', I often feel not happiness, pleasure, delight but a choking sensation. I realized that the meaning of love is similar to that of an adverb 'nevertheless.' What makes me happy, glad, thankful nevertheless when I feel tired and exhausted. I believe that it is love. I hope that you will take comfort from my illustrations which consoled me.

깜짝 놀라겠지!

두근두근!

I bet he'll be surprised!

Ba-bum. Ba-bum!

여 유 로 운
오 후

한가한 오후.

책을 읽어요. :)

Serene afternoon

On a quiet afternoon, We read books. :)

Get out
Garfield!

말썽꾸러기
가필드가
자꾸 주방에 들어와요!

Get out, Garfield!

Silly Garfield keeps coming into the kitchen!

Wake up

창가에 누워 책을 읽다 잠이 들었습니다.
"일어나세요."

Wake up

I fell asleep while reading by the window. "Wake up."

Tea time

따뜻한 오후, 차를 마시며 휴식을 취합니다.

Tea time

On a warm afternoon, we drink tea as we relax.

작
업
실　작은 작업실 안에서 각자의 시간을 즐깁니다.

The studio

We each enjoy our time in the small studio.

양
치

함께 양치를 합니다.
구석구석 깨끗이 치카치카!

Brushing teeth

We brush our teeth together. Fresh and clean!

거 리 에 서

한 입만….

On the street

Give me a bite.

포
코
팡
!

휴대폰 게임을 즐기며 여유를 만끽합니다.

"내가 이기면 소원 두 개 들어주는 거야!"

Poco Pang!

We enjoy our spare time playing mobile games. "If I win, grant me two wishes, okay?"

너를 그려 줄게

"지금 그대로 가만히 있어야 해."

평화로운 오후,

마주 앉아 서로를 바라보며 시간을 보냅니다. :)

I will draw your portrait

"Stay still."

Calm afternoon, We sit face to face and spend our time looking at one another. :)

아 침 해 가 떴 는 데 도

'코야' 해요….

Even when the morning sun comes up

Zzz….

눈
싸
움

온 세상을 하얗게 뒤덮은 겨울.

밖에 나와 신나게 눈싸움을 합니다.

"나 진짜 화났어. 거기 가만히 있어!"

Snowball fight

When the world is coated white in the winter, We step outside to have a snow fight.

"I'm serious. Stay right where you are!"

심 야
영 화

모두가 잠든 깊은 밤.
소파에 앉아 과자를 먹으며 공포 영화에 빠져듭니다.
와그작와그작!

Movie night

Everyone is sound asleep.

We eat snacks and sink into a scary movie on the sofa.

Crunch, crunch!

낮
잠

주말 오후, 테라스 의자에 기대어 낮잠을 잡니다.

노곤노곤~

Nap time

On a weekend afternoon, we take a nap leaning on the terrace sofa. Zzz....

앞 머 리 쯤 이 야 내 가 할 수 있 지 !

걱정 말아요! 내가 멋지게 잘라줄게!

C'mon, I can cut your bangs!

Don't worry! I'll make you handsome!

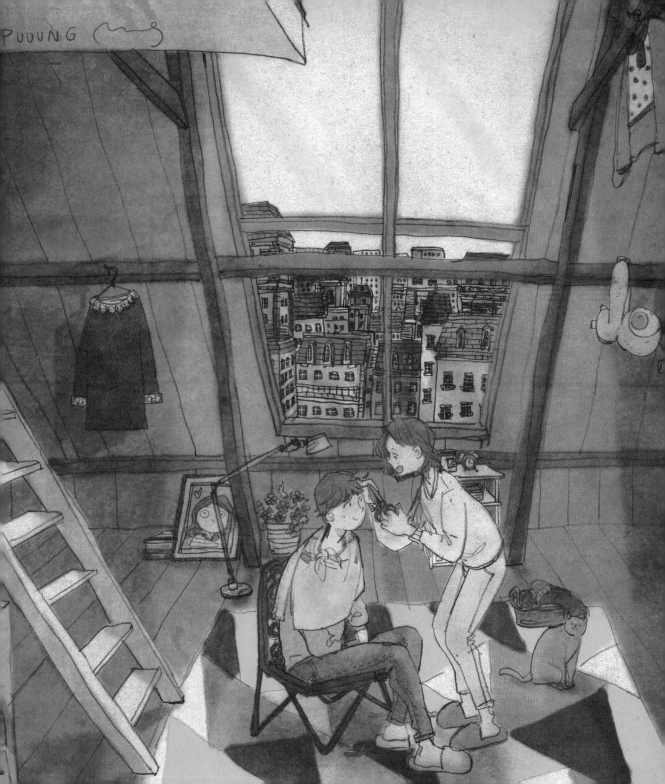

카
메
라

여기 보세요~ 찰칵!

Camera

Look over here. Click!

쪽 잠

피곤을 못 이기고
엎드려 잠든 여자에게 담요를 덮어줍니다.
이렇게 자면 감기 걸려요.

Catnap

Couldn't help her sleepiness,
The girl fell asleep on her desk.
He covers her with a blanket.
You'll catch a cold sleeping like this.

설 거 지 당 번

"이겼다!"

"그냥 식기세척기 하나 사면 안 돼?"

Who's turn is it to do the dishes?

"I won!" "Can't we just buy a dishwasher?"

타
버
렸
어   음식이 시커멓게 타버렸습니다.

맛있는 음식을 기다리는 남자의 모습에

여자의 마음도 시커멓게 타들어갑니다.

It burned

The food burned to a crisp.

Looking at him patiently waiting for a delicious meal, Her heart also burns to a crisp.

첨 벙 첨 벙

물놀이를 해요.

Splish-splash

We play in the water.

볼
말 랑 말 랑

말랑말랑한 볼을 꾹 누르며
애정 표현을 합니다.

Squeezing cheeks

Squeezing her squishy cheeks, He shows sweet affection for her.

요 리

피크닉을 가기 위해
함께 도시락을 만듭니다.
"자, 잘 봐. 뒤집는다!"

Cooking

To go on a picnic,
We prepare food together.
"Look at me, I'm going to flip it!"

정
원

주말 오후, 정원에 앉아 이야기를 나눕니다.

"나른하다, 그치?"

Garden

On a weekend afternoon, they have a chat in a garden. "Growing sleepy, yeah?"

잡
담

책상 앞에서의 사소한 이야기들.

"이것만 끝나면 '트레이더스' 가는 거야, 알았지?"

Small talk

They chat about small things by the desk. "After this one, we're going to Trader's, okay?"

늦은
점심

느긋하게 시간을 보내다가 밥때를 놓쳐버렸습니다.
늦은 점심은 배달 음식으로 해결하기로 결정합니다.
"라지 피자 두 판 배달 부탁드려요."

Late lunch

We lost track of time and missed lunch. We decide to order food.
"I'd like to order two large pizzas, please."

캠 핑 카 에 서

맛있는 음료 만들어줄게요!
짹짹이랑 놀고 있어요!

In a camping car

I'll make you something to drink!
In the meantime, play with Birdy!

뒹굴뒹굴

딱히 하는 일 없이 뒹굴뒹굴.

Lolling around

Lolling around with nothing
particular to do.

트 렌 치 코 트

트렌치코트를 입고

나들이 가고픈 계절이 왔어요. :)

Trench coat

The season has arrived when we want to wear trench coats and go out. :)

일
어
나

일어나요.
자, 안아줘!

Wake up

Wake up. Now, give me hug!

벚 나 무
밑 에 서

옆으로 더 붙어요.
자, 찍을게!

Underneath the cherry blossom tree

Come closer. Ready, cheese!

보
드
게
임

설거지 벌칙이 걸린 무시무시한 게임!
숨죽이고 온 신경을 집중해요!

Board game

A terrifying game to decide who will do the dishes!
You better focus!

수 고 했 어

오늘 하루도 수고했어.

일을 끝마치고 해 질 녘에 마시는 차 한잔.

Good job

You did a good job today, like always. A cup of tea after work as the sun sets.

공 부

시험 기간,
같은 책상에 앉아 각자 공부를 해요.
네가 옆에 있는데 어떻게 집중을 하지?

Studying

During the exam week,
We sit together and each study on our own.
How can I concentrate when you're beside me?

오 늘
점 심 은 뭐 예 요 ?

"오늘 점심은 뭐예요?"
"볶음밥!"

What's for lunch today?

"What's for lunch today?" "Fried rice!"

081

바 쁜 날

아침밥은커녕 깨워주지도 못하고 나가는 바쁜 날.

Busy day

Hardly had time to wake him up, let alone make breakfast.

이불은 덮고 자요

감기 걸리겠다….

Cover yourself with a blanket

Or you'll catch a cold.

더
워

"더워서 아무것도 하기 싫다…."

"나도…."

So hot

"It's so hot, I don't want to do anything."

"Me neither."

음 식
만 드 는 걸
구 경 해 요

아침 맛있게 해줄게!

Watching him cook

I'll make you a tasty breakfast!

한
가
한

오
후

여유로운 날.

Laid-back afternoon

An easy going day.

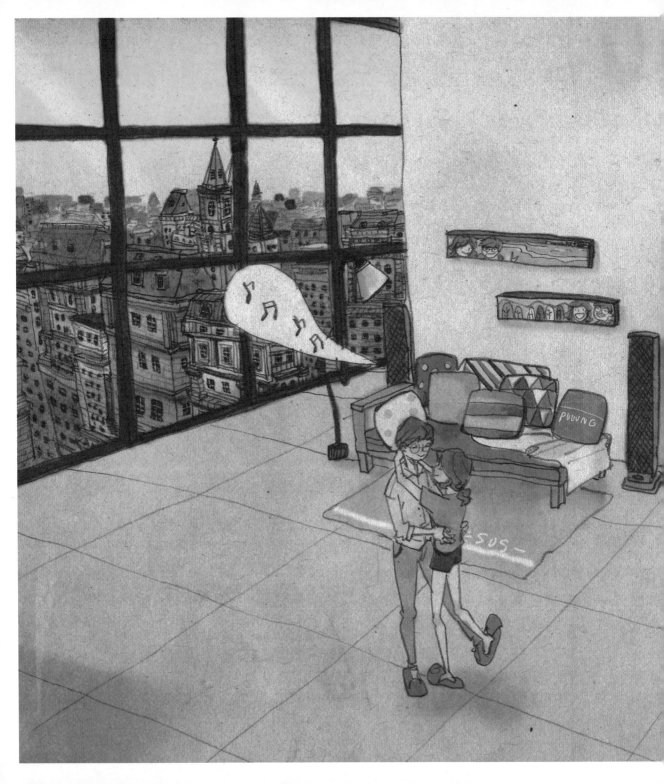

춤

같이 춤춰요.

Dance

Dance with me.

무 서 운
꿈 을
꿨 어

많이 무서웠어?
괜찮아.
내가 옆에 있잖아.

I had a scary dream

Was it really scary?

It's okay. I'm here with you.

장 보 기

어떤 걸 살까?

Grocery shopping

Which one should we get?

미 안 해 !

정말 미안해! T_T

I'm sorry

I'm really sorry! T_T

해 질 녘 생 각

너 없을 때도 네 생각.

A thought at sunset

I think about you even when you're not there.

누 워 서 1

가끔은 아무것도 하지 않고 누워서
그냥 쉬고 싶을 때가 있어.

Lying down I

Sometimes we just want to lie down
and not do anything.

누워서 2

그냥 누워서.

Lying down II

Just lying down.

가
끔
은

가끔은 아무것도 안 하고, 그 누구도 대면하지 않고
혼자 누워 있고 싶을 때가 있어.

Sometimes

Sometimes I don't want to do anything, nor talk to anyone.

I just want to lie down alone.

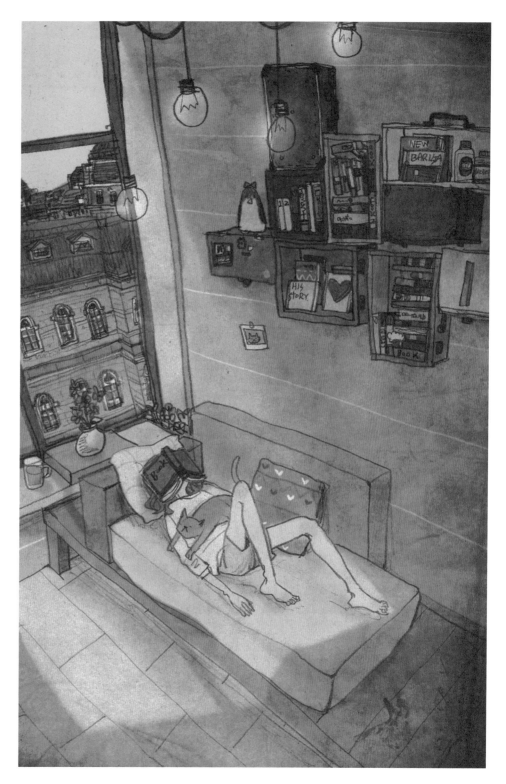

느긋한
아침
준비

오늘은 천천히.
이야기하면서 아침을 차려요.

Taking time to prepare breakfast

No rush today, We make breakfast while indulging in conversation.

자꾸만 안고 싶은 걸 어떡해요

사랑스러운 당신.

I can't help wanting to hold you

Lovely you.

예쁜
노래를
불러 줘요

음정도 박자도 모두 엉터리지만
그마저도 사랑스러워요.

Sing me a pretty song

She sings terribly out tune and rhythm,
But even so she is loveable.

앨 범
정 리

우리의 추억이 이렇게나 많이 쌓였어요!

Putting photos in an album

Look at all these memories we've made!

홈
파 티

오늘은 친구들도 함께해요. :)

Home gathering

Today, our friends join us. :)

가 필 드
목 욕 을
시 켜 요

괜찮아, 무서운 거 아냐!
이제 다 끝났어!

Giving Garfield a bath

It's okay, there's nothing to be scared of!
We're done!

뜨끈뜨끈
백숙
요리

백숙을 해 먹어요!
"어때 간 맞아?"

Steamy chicken soup

We make a pot of chicken soup!

"How does it taste?"

어떤 케이크가 좋아?

모르겠어. 달콤한 거면 다 좋아.

Which cake do you like?

I don't know. I like anything sweet.

잘
다
녀
와
요
!

눈길 조심하고 잘 다녀와요!

See you later!

Be careful on the snowy roads and be safe!

창 가 에 앉 아 서

Sitting by the window

크 리 스 마 스 트 리 를 꾸 며 요

함께 크리스마스트리를 꾸며요.

"이거 이렇게 감는 거 맞아?"

"응응! 내가 금방 내려갈게!"

Decorating the Christmas tree

We decorate the Christmas tree together.

"Is this how you string the lights?"

"Yep yep! I'll be right there!"

빨 리
와 요 !

언제 도착해요?
진짜진짜
맛있는 거 만들고 있으니까
빨리 와요!

Hurry back!

When will you be here?
I'm making something
Really really tasty
So hurry back!

오 늘
날 씨
많 이 춥 대 요 !

오늘 날씨는 많이 춥대요.
따뜻하게 입고 가야겠다!

It says it's quite chilly today!

Today's weather seems very cold. You better bundle up!

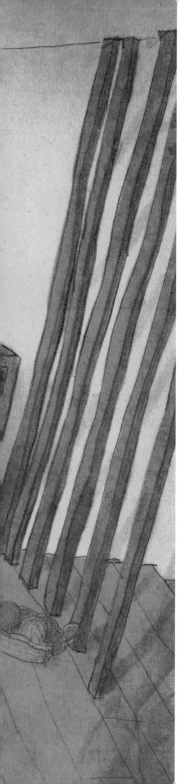

머 리 묶 어 줄 게 요

예쁘게 묶어주세요!

I'll tie your hair

Make it pretty!

뽀 뽀

그 어떤 것보다 효과 좋은 피로 회복제예요!

A peck

There's no better cure for fatigue!

조 물
조 물

조물조물 클레이로 만들기를 해요!

두 사람은 아이처럼 클레이 놀이에 푹 빠져서

투정을 부리기도 했어요.

"만들기는 못하겠어. 너무 어려워요…."

"잘 못 만들어도 괜찮아요. 잘 봐!"

Clay craft

They make some clay crafts with their hands.

Like kids, the two dived into crafting fun And he started whining.

"I can't do this. It's too difficult…"

"It doesn't have to be perfect. Look!"

외 출 전

신발 끈이 풀렸어요.

내가 묶어줄게요!

Getting ready to go out

Your shoelaces are untied. I'll tie them for you!

꼭

껴 안 고

자 요

이보다 더 포근한 꿈나라 여행은 없을 거예요!

We hug tightly and sleep

There can't be a dream cozier than this!

창 밖 을
바 라 보 며

함께 창밖을 바라봤어요.

이 세상에 나와 너뿐인 게 아니에요.

이 아름다운 세상 속에 너와 내가 있어요!

Looking out the window

We gazed out the window together.

You and I are not alone in this world.

You and I are living in this beautiful world.

손 잡 고
걸 어 요

손잡고 거리를 걸어요.

Holding hands and walking together

We hold hands as we walk down the streets.

울
지
마

미안해, 울지 말아요.
얼굴 들어봐, 예쁜 얼굴 좀 보여줘요.

Don't cry

I'm sorry, don't cry.

Raise your head, and let me see your pretty face.

기 다 렸 어 요

"춥게 왜 밖에서 기다리고 있었어?"

"언제 오나 해서!"

"귀 차가운 것 좀 봐, 많이 추웠지?"

I waited for you

"It's cold, why are you waiting outside?"

"I didn't know when you'd be back!"

"Your ears are so cold, you must be freezing!"

빙
그
르
르

장난스럽게 손을 잡고 춤을 췄어요.

Twirling

We held hands and playfully danced.

숲
속 의
도 서 관

숲 속의 도서관에서 책을 읽어요.

집중하지 못하고 그새 장난을 쳐요.

사랑해! 하트 뿅뿅!

A library in the forest

We read books at a library in the forest.

Unable to concentrate, we are quick to joke around.

I love you! Heart, heart!

휴 대 폰 게 임

소파에 앉아서 함께 휴대폰 게임을 해요.

사소한 일이지만 이마저도 행복해요.

Mobile game

We sit on the sofa together and play mobile games.

We find happiness even in the smallest of things.

가 던 길 에
멈 춰 서 서

가던 길에 멈춰 서서, 쪽!
향기가 참 좋아서 이대로 놔주고 싶지가 않아요.

Stopping on the way

I stop on the way, and smooch!
Your fragrance makes it hard for me to let you go.

테 이 블 앞 에 서
마 주 보 고

마주 보고 이야기를 나눠요.

At the table

We look at each other and have a conversation.

편안한
대화

푹신푹신한 이불 위에서 과자를 먹으며 이야기를 나눠요.

Comfortably conversing

On the soft blankets, we eat snacks and converse.

간 식
드 세 요 !

"맛있는 핫케이크 먹으면서 하세요."
"고마워요!"

Here's your snack

"Have some pancakes while you're working." "Thank you!"

전 화
통 화

정말정말 보고 싶어요.

"맛있는 거 사 갈게요. 조금만 기다려요!"

Phone call

I miss you so, so much. "I'll bring something delicious. Wait a little longer!"

테 이 블 에   낙 서 하 는   식 당

테이블 위에 낙서하는 레스토랑에 왔어요.

최고의 외식이에요!

Doodling on the restaurant table

We came to a restaurant where we can doodle on the table. This is the best!

봄

봄이 왔어요!

수많은 벚꽃과 살랑살랑 봄바람 그리고 눈앞의 당신!

가슴이 울렁울렁해요.

Spring

Spring has arrived! Countless cherry blossoms, a gentle breeze, and you! My heart flutters.

소 소 한
이 벤 트

깜짝 이벤트!

작은 부엌은 우리만의 특별한 레스토랑이 됐어요.

"메인 요리 나왔습니다. 맛있게 드세요!"

A little something

Surprise! The small kitchen became our special restaurant. "Your main dish is here. Bon appetit!"

책 을 읽 어 줘 요 1

너의 목소리를 들으며 잠들어요.

Read to me I

I fall asleep listening to your voice.

도
서
관

앗, 조심해요!

높은 책장에서 책을 꺼내다가 넘어질 뻔했어요!

Library

Woah, be careful! You almost fell while taking out a book from the highshelf!

비
오
는
날

우르릉 쾅쾅! 무섭게 번개가 쳐요!
오늘 같은 날씨는 정말 무서워요….

Rainy day

Boom, boom! The lightning is frightening! Weather Like this is very scary.

자 전 거

따르릉따르릉! 자전거를 타고 함께 거리를 달려요!

Bicycle

Ting-a-ring! We ride bikes down the streets.

자 꾸 만
바 라 보 게
돼 요

네가 뒤에 있으니까 자꾸 돌아보게 돼요. 전혀 집중할 수가 없어요!

Can't stop looking at you

I keep looking back because you're behind me. I can't concentrate at all!

계
단
에
서

계단에 걸터앉은 널 계속 바라봤어요.

그렇게 계속 보면 뽀뽀해버릴 거예요!

On the stairs

I kept looking at you sitting on the edge of the stairs.

If you keep looking at me like that, I will kiss you!

책 을 읽 어 줘 요 2

누워서 책 읽어주는 소리를 들어요.
내용엔 전혀 집중하지 않았어요.
그냥 네 예쁜 목소리만 느껴요!

Read to me II

I hear you reading to me as I lie down.

I don't pay attention to the book at all. I just listen to your pretty voice!

어 부 바

다리 많이 아프죠? 내가 어부바해줄게요!

나 엄청 힘세요!

Piggyback

Are your legs okay? I'll give you a piggyback ride! I'm super strong!

놀러 갈
계획을 짜요

"이번 여름에는 어디로 놀러 갈까?"
"어디 가고 싶어요?"
너랑 같이 가는 거라면 어디든지 다 좋아!

Planning a vacation

"Where should we go this summer?"

"Where do you want to go?"

I don't care as long as you're there!

이 불 빨 래

폭신폭신 이불 빨래를 해요.

힘든 집안일도 너랑 같이 하면 재밌어요!

Laundry

We wash a fluffy comforter. Even tedious chores are fun when I'm with you!

별 을
구 경 해 요

테라스에 앉아서 별을 구경해요.

Stargazing

We stargaze sitting on the terrace.

소
소
한 잡
담

내일이면 잘 기억하지도 못할 아주 소소한 잡담.

Chit-chat

Chatting about things we won't even remember tomorrow.

치 킨
사 왔 어

짜잔! 치킨 사 왔어!
우아! 최고최고! XD

I brought fried chicken

Tada! I brought fried chicken!
Wow! You're the best! XD

너 에 게 로 가 는 길

너에게로 가는 길은 얼마나 즐거운 길인지 몰라요!

멀지도, 지루하게 느껴지지도 않아요.

저 멀리서 네가 손 흔드는 모습이 보여요.

자꾸만 웃음이 새어 나와요!

On the way to you

I can't express how happy I am when I'm on my way to see you!

It doesn't feel far or boring at all. I see you waving way over there.

I can't stop smiling!

푹 신 푹 신

나만을 위한 침대!
언제나 내 곁에 있지요.

Soft and cozy

A bed just for me! Always there by my side.

외
출

꽃도 사고 쇼핑도 했어요.

이제 집에 갈까요?

Going out

We bought flowers and other things. Shall we go home now?

꽃
아 래 에 서

뽀뽀하고 싶어요.

Beneath the flowers

I want to kiss you.

친 구 들 이
놀 러 왔 어 요

친구들이 놀러 왔어요.
고요했던 둘만의 공간이 시끌벅적해졌어요!

Our friends came over

Our friends came over. Our quiet place became noisy!

더
운
밤

더운 밤. 밖에 나와서 반짝반짝 불꽃놀이를 즐겨요.

"너무 예쁘다. 누구 스파클러가 먼저 꺼질까?"

"꺼지지 않았으면 좋겠어. 지금 이대로 시간이 흐르지 않았으면 좋겠어!"

Hot summer night

Hot Summer night. We step outside and light sparklers.

"So pretty. Whose sparkler will finish first?"

"I don't want them to end. I wish time would stop right now!"

당구를
쳐요

치킨 사 오기 내기를 건 왕초보들의 포켓볼 대결!
승자는 과연 누구…?!

Playing pool

A bet between two amateurs on who will buy fried chicken!
And the winner is….

그 리 고

또 다 른 이 야 기 들

And Other stories

도서관에서 건축 관련 서적을 보면서
작품 속 공간을 구상했습니다.

Reading architectural books in a library,
I conceived the spaces in my works.

그 공간 속에서
캐릭터들이 어떤 행동을 할지
상상하면서 에피소드를 만들었지요.

And I made episodes,
imagining what my characters do there.

제가 애용하는 연필이에요.
코팅이 되어 있지 않아
누드 연필이라고 불러요.

These are the pencils that
I love to use.
There are uncoated.
So I call them nude pencils.